HOW THE WITCH GOT ALF

by Cora Annett

illustrated by Steven Kellogg

A Noodle Factory Children's Book Club
Presentation

FRANKLIN WATTS | NEW YORK | LONDON

1975

Library of Congress Cataloging in Publication Data

Annett, Cora.
    How the witch got Alf.

      SUMMARY: Alf, the donkey, takes drastic
measures to find out that he is loved as much as
the old folks' other animals.
      [1. Donkeys—Fiction] I. Kellogg, Steven, illus.
II. Title.
PZ7.A5867Ho   [E]   74-8808
ISBN 0-531-02791-0

For all
(un)lovable donkeys,
everywhere

Nobody noticed when Alf the Donkey began grumbling to himself. Indeed, no one ever noticed Alf at all. And that was just the trouble! He did his work around the farm every day. He took the Old Man and the Old Woman to the village in the wagon once each week so that they could do their buying and selling. And in return he was given his daily hay. And that was that.

But the Dog and the Cat and the Canary—well! There was a different story.

The Canary did nothing but sit and sing all day. And as a reward for that the Old Woman put special treats inside his cage. She whistled to him and called him sweet names and made silly faces at him.

The Cat could come and go as she liked. And for doing nothing she got saucers of cream. She sat on the Old Woman's lap and had her fine silky fur stroked. At night she slept at the foot of the Old Folks' bed.

The Dog liked to think that he was taking care of the farm, guarding it at night. But in reality, Alf knew, he did nothing. Yet the Old Man was always praising him. They played together in the yard, the Dog leaping upon the Old Man and trying to lick his face. And the Old Man would laugh and scratch the Dog's ears.

For Alf it was work, work, work, all the time, and never any play.

At night they all slept in the warm cozy cottage. But Alf—the cold barn was good enough for *him*.

One evening in spring, Alf watched from his stall in the barn as the Old Man and the Dog played in the yard. Through the cottage door he could see the Cat purring contentedly in the Old Woman's lap as she sat knitting. He could hear the Canary filling the air with his song. And Alf grew bitter.

"Ha!" he snorted. "What do I care?"

He turned completely around in his stall to show how much he did not care, and stood there looking at the wall.

"Not a single, teensy-weensy bit do I care," he said. "I don't care a fig. Or a Fig Newton either. Not even an apple."

But Alf could still hear the Canary singing.

"And what's so marvelous in that?" he asked himself. "A donkey could sing as well. I, Alf, could sing as well!"

Then he shifted his hooves about in a sheepish sort of way. "I've just never tried, that's all," he muttered. "But I certainly *could*," he said after a while, "...if I wanted to."

He lifted his head and a little gleam crept into his eye. "Yes, why not?" He turned around in his stall again. "Why, when you don't like the way things are going, you do something to change them! *That's* what you do!" he said aloud to the empty barn. (Only it came out sounding like "Ee-*yonk*, ee-*yonk*, ee-*yonk*!")

He was excited because he had suddenly thought of a plan for changing things, and he just *knew* it would work. But it had to wait until morning. He settled himself down in the straw and went over and over in his mind what he was going to do. And at last he went to sleep.

Bright and early the next morning he jumped up and danced happily across the farmyard to the cottage. He sat down outside the open bedroom window of the Old People.

This morning *he* would sing them awake. He—Alf—instead of that insufferable Canary.

"Ee-*yonk*!" he began loudly and joyously, breaking the stillness of the early morning air. "Ee-*yonk*, ee-*yonk*!"

The Old Man rose up out of bed as if an explosion had been set off under him.

"My heavens!" he gasped. "What *is* that?"

The Old Woman, still sleepy-eyed, stumbling over her nightgown, rushed to the window.

"Why, it's Alf," she said in wonder.

"Alf!" said the Old Man. "What's got into him? Has he gone mad?"

Alf went on serenading with all his heart. He threw back his head and closed his eyes and sang as sweetly as he knew how. "Ee-*yonk*, ee-yo-*honk*."

But the Old Woman did not whistle to him. She did not call him sweet names, or give him a treat. She looked completely dumbfounded.

"Wait, *I'll* give him something," said the Old Man.

"Ah, at last!" thought Alf, and he continued to sing even louder and more joyously, in gratitude.

What Alf got was a bucketful of water poured over his head.

"*That* will cure him of his crazy spell," said the Old Man as he slammed the window shut.

Alf shook his head, partly to get the water out of his eyes and ears and partly because he was puzzled. Slowly he trotted back to the barn, where he spent the rest of the morning thinking deeply about the matter.

Finally he said, "Well, perhaps a canary *can* sing better than a donkey." He would just have to think up a new plan.

But he could not think of one, though he spent the rest of the day trying. In the evening, when he saw the Old Man standing alone in the yard waiting for supper to be ready, an idea came to Alf like a shot. And like a shot Alf rushed from his stall, galloped gleefully across the yard, threw himself upon the Old Man—as he had seen the Dog do so often—and began eagerly licking the Old Man's face.

But the Old Man did not laugh and scratch Alf's ears. Instead, he staggered backward with a look of dismay, throwing his arms up in front of his head.

"Pfaugh!" he said, pushing the Donkey away. "Are you really mad, then? This is too much. Down! Down, you wild thing!"

Alf got down, perplexed. He backed away and looked at the Old Man for a moment. Then he turned around and trotted slowly back to the barn, shaking his head in bewilderment.

And the Old Man went into the cottage, shaking *his* head, and saying to the Old Woman, "I think a witch must have put a spell on Alf, he is acting in such a crazy way."

In his stall, Alf tried to figure out what he had done wrong. At last he gave up. He would just have to make a new plan.

But again he could not think of anything—not until the next morning when he was nibbling at tufts of grass in the barnyard, and he looked up to see the Old Woman through the cottage door, as she sat down in her rocking chair to take a moment's rest. Then all at once an idea came to Alf. He looked quickly about. The accursed Cat was nowhere to be seen. Now was his chance!

Eagerly he loped across the yard, trotted right through the cottage door, and sat himself down in the Old Woman's lap. He did his best to purr.

But did the Old Woman stroke his fine silky fur? Not a bit! She fell backward in her chair, screaming to high heaven.

The Old Man came running in from the lettuce patch to see what was the matter. When he saw Alf he grabbed the kitchen mop and chased Alf all the way into the barn.

Then he went back to the cottage and said to his wife, "He is mad for certain! Tomorrow we will have the doctor come and look at him."

In his stall, Alf hung his head and heaved a sigh. He was sad and thoughtful.

When a dog plays with someone he gets his ears scratched. But not a donkey.

When a cat climbs onto someone's lap she gets petted and pampered. But not a donkey.

When a canary sings he gets nice things to eat. But not a donkey.

Alf walked down to the duck pond and looked at his reflection in the water. Perhaps his ears were too long and floppy. The Dog's ears were short and smart-looking. And perhaps his coat was too rough and dry. The Cat's coat was fine and silky. And his voice—well, the less said about it, the better. He certainly did not have the voice of a canary.

"A donkey is not lovable," he decided. "That's all."

And then Alf made up his mind to run away.

At first he was going to go far, far away to another land. Across the ocean. Then he thought, well, he didn't have to go all *that* far. Maybe just to the next town. Then he thought that wasn't really necessary either. Maybe he could run away to someplace close by, so he could see what happened after he left.

And suddenly he thought of the perfect spot.

That night, after everyone had gone to bed, and everything was dark and silent, Alf made his way quickly across the farmyard to the cottage. There, he leaped upon a barrel that stood next to the house. From the barrel, he jumped upon the low roof overhanging the porch. And from there, he clambered up onto the roof of the house.

Of course, all of this made a great deal of noise.

The Old Man and the Old Woman awoke from a sound sleep and jumped out of bed in terror.

"The house is caving in!" cried the Old Woman.

"It's a tornado!" cried the Old Man.

"The earth is opening up to swallow us—house, farm, and all!" shrieked the Old Woman.

"It's an earthquake!" shouted the Old Man.

But by then the racket had stopped, and they saw that none of these terrible things was really happening.

"We must be calm," said the Old Man. "The noise came from the roof."

He put his head out the window and peered upward.

What he saw was Alf huddling stock-still, with one ear pointed toward the sky, trying not to be seen.

But the Old Man did not know it was Alf. All he saw was a shadowy figure with a pointed thing on its head. The Old Man shuddered and quickly closed the window and locked it.

"Come, wife," he whispered. "Let us go to bed and
to sleep. It's a witch up there. No doubt she stopped
on our roof to rest. We will forget all about it. In the
morning she will surely be gone." And they went to bed
and to sleep, clinging to each other in fright.

After that, Alf was careful not to make any noise.
He settled himself in toward the center of the roof,
where he could not be seen, and was quite pleased
with himself for having found the perfect hiding place
for a runaway donkey.

The next morning the Old Man walked around
outside the cottage looking up at the roof until he was
satisfied that the witch had gone.

It did not take him long to find out that Alf was
also gone.

The Old Man and the Old Woman ran all over the farm, searching for him and calling his name. But no flop-eared little donkey trotted eagerly to them. No familiar "Ee-*yonk*" answered their calls.

Alf, watching and listening from his hiding place, enjoyed all this immensely. He was only disappointed that they gave up searching for him so soon.

"Well, no matter," he said, arranging himself comfortably. "I shall simply stay here forever."

He heard the Old Folks going into the cottage.

"They will never see me or hear from me again," he said with satisfaction.

He listened to them moving about inside.

"Of course, I will pine away from starvation," Alf said cheerfully.

He lifted his head and nibbled at some leaves from a tree whose branches hung over the roof.

"Someday they will come up here and find a pile of old bones. And that's all that will be left of old Alf," he said contentedly.

He rested his head on his front hooves and gazed dreamily off into the distance.

"And won't they be sorry!" The thought gave him a funny little excited feeling. "I can hardly wait to see their faces *then!*" he said.

Inside the cottage it was very quiet. The Old Man and the Old Woman hardly spoke as they ate their supper. They went to bed that night without a word. The next morning they ate their breakfast in silence. Indeed, they hardly felt like eating at all.

They did not set briskly about their chores as they usually did every morning. Instead, the Old Woman sat down in her rocking chair, but she did not rock. And the Old Man stood in the doorway looking out, but he did not see anything.

The Canary sang, but no one paid him any attention.

The Cat leaped up on the Old Woman's lap and began purring. But the Old Woman only sat gazing through the window and did not move.

The Dog pranced about in the yard, hoping his master would come out and play with him. But the Old Man did not even notice him.

At last the Old Woman spoke. "It must have been that witch that got our Alf."

"Yes, yes, it must be so," agreed the Old Man. "Why else would he have disappeared in the dark of night?"

"Poor Alf," said the Old Woman. And she sighed. After a moment she asked in a hushed voice, "What do you suppose she'll do with him?"

The Old Man shuddered. "Better not to think of it."

"Ah, poor Alf," said the Old Woman. "We'll never see our little Donkey again." And she began to weep.

The Old Man sighed deeply. "Never."

"Do you remember how eagerly he used to come when we called, going 'Ee-yonk, ee-yonk' all the while?" said the Old Woman. "How fond he was of us."

"A good little creature," said the Old Man. "Always did his work, never complained."

"So cheerfully he pulled us to market in the wagon. So patiently he waited all day in the hot sun while we did our buying and selling."

"Poor Alf," said the Old Man. And again he sighed, wiping his eyes.

The Canary stopped his chirping and singing and gazed sorrowfully through the bars of his cage. The Cat stopped purring and lay with her head drooping dolefully between her paws. The Dog stopped prancing and gave a sad little whine.

"We shall miss our little Donkey," said the Old Man.

"Our dear Donkey," said the Old Woman.

As Alf lay listening to all of this, something strange was going on inside him. He enjoyed hearing the nice things they were saying about him, to be sure. He had not known what a good donkey he was, and he was quite pleased to find it out. But at the same time he was beginning to feel very, very sad. He felt sorry for the poor lost Donkey. He felt sorry for the poor Old Folks who would never see their dear Donkey again.

In fact, he began to feel so sad that large tears rolled down his long nose and off the edge of the roof, splashing upon the sill outside the window where the Old Woman sat.

She saw the drops falling. "See, even the heavens are weeping with us," she said. "It's raining."

"Raining?" said the Old Man. "But the sun is shining here in the yard."

His wife was not listening. She was crying harder than ever.

Then the Dog began to howl, the Cat began to yowl, the Canary hiccuped, the Old Woman wailed, and the Old Man began to sob.

This was almost too much for Alf. He nearly decided to come down, right then and there. But he remembered that he had made up his mind to run away forever. So instead, he gave a determined snort and settled himself more firmly in place and tried not to hear the racket down below.

The next day was a long, weary one for Alf. A deep gloom seemed to have settled over the house. There was not a single peep out of the Canary, not a yip out of the Dog, or a mew out of the Cat. The Old People were not wailing and crying anymore, but they were not saying nice things about Alf either, which he found quite annoying. They just went about doing their work, because the work had to be done, Donkey or no Donkey, and one can't sit moping all day.

Alf grew bored. By midmorning he had eaten all the leaves off the overhanging branch, just for something to do. Then at noon the hot sun beat down upon him, and because the leaves were gone, there was no shade to protect him. He could do nothing but lie there in the heat, hoping for a little breeze that never came.

By the end of the day he was beginning to get very hungry because, with the leaves all gone, there was nothing more to eat. And on top of everything else, he was thirsty and he was getting tired of sitting still.

"Well," he thought to himself. "One must expect a few hardships when one runs away forever. It can't be helped."

The next day was much the same, except that Alf was now very, *very* hungry, and very, *very* thirsty, and very, *very* tired of sitting in one place, and very, *very* bored. How good a mouthful of hay would taste right now! How fine it would feel if he could just frisk about the yard a bit to stretch his legs. He lay on his back and kicked his legs in the air to get some exercise. But this only made him hungrier than ever, so he had to stop.

And everything below was still and silent. The Old Man was off plowing in the field. The only sound to be heard was the Old Woman at her work in the cottage.

Then Alf began to think about the future. What would happen tomorrow? Nothing, very likely. It would be a day just like today. And so would the next day, and the next day, and the next day. . . . In fact, as far as he could see, every day would be just like today, for weeks, months, years, even — with nothing ever happening, while he went on sitting right here on the roof. Alf gave a shudder. What an awful thought!

Now if he had some company, that might help a bit. If only the Canary would sing again. There was something so cheerful about his singing. It had made Alf's heart glad. And for the first time, he realized that the Canary had his own job—just as a donkey did—and that job was to brighten everyone's spirits.

If only the Cat would come and sit next to him, purring, as she used to do when she visited him sometimes in the barn. If only the Dog would play in the yard again. It used to make Alf laugh to watch his antics.

Why had he been angry with them, anyway? For a moment he could not remember. Ah, yes. It was because they did not work as hard as he did. But Alf knew that he had not been really fair. For the Cat kept the house and barn free of mice, and the Dog did keep watch on things—no fox ever got at the chickens while he was around.

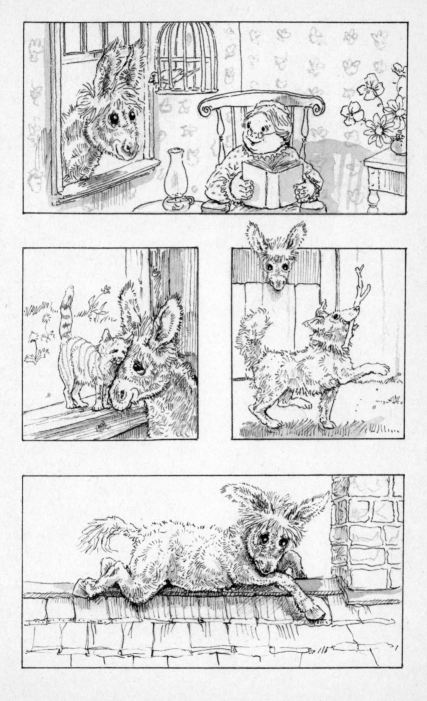

Well, Alf admitted to himself, he had been wrong. And he certainly did miss everyone. And he badly wanted things to be back as they used to be. Of course, all he had to do was to come down off the roof and everything would be the same again. But to come down off the roof was impossible, for he had run away forever.

Just then the Old Man came in from the fields. He was hot and tired, and he was cross besides, because he had had to push the plow by himself all day long with no donkey to help him.

"It is time to forget Alf now," he told his wife when she met him at the door. "Tomorrow I am going to buy a new donkey."

"Yes, I think you are right," she answered. "One can't go on mourning an old donkey forever."

At that, the Canary gave a tiny, hopeful chirp. The Cat got up and stretched and began chasing a butterfly. The Dog pranced a bit about the yard, then went off to hunt rabbits. And the Old Folks went into the cottage to eat their supper.

Right then, Alf decided that he had been gone long enough. It was time to come down off the roof.

But horrors! When he started down, how far away the ground seemed! It made him dizzy just to look. With that first step, he began slipping and sliding in a most alarming way.

He sat a long time, wondering what to do. Should he lie on his back and slide down? Wouldn't he land with an awful bump? Should he just take a running leap over the side? No, somehow that did not seem wise.

He thought and thought until it was quite dark and the Old People had gone to bed, but he could not think of a way to get down.

Then it began to rain. And the wind began to blow. The Old Folks in their bed listened to the wind howling and whistling about the cottage.

"It's a night for witches," the Old Man whispered to the Old Woman. They snuggled deeper under their warm blankets.

Poor Alf! He was hungry. He ached from sitting still in one place. He was lonesome. And now he was wet and miserable on top of everything else.

"Ee-*yonk*!" he called, hoping the Old Folks would come and rescue him. "Ee-*yonk*! Ee-*yonk*!"

But the wind picked up his forlorn cry and flung it off across the fields.

"Funny," the Old Woman murmured drowsily. "I thought I heard Alf calling from far, far away."

"You are only dreaming," said the Old Man. "It is the wind."

And they went to sleep.

34

As the night wore on, the wind grew stronger and stronger. It blew so hard that Alf had all he could do to keep from being blown off the roof. It blew him this way and that. His hooves bumped and scraped as he tried to keep his footing. At last he wrapped his front legs around the chimney, and that helped some.

But the noise he made through all this woke up the Old Folks.

They lay in their bed gazing wide-eyed at the ceiling, listening to the bumping and scraping. And they trembled.

"What do you suppose it is?" the Old Man whispered.

"You said it's a night for witches," the Old Woman whispered back.

"Yes?"

"Maybe—maybe witches are dancing on the roof."

"Ah!"

They were silent a few minutes.

"Well, aren't you going to do something about it?" asked the Old Woman.

"Do what? What is there to do?"

"Scare them away. We can't have witches dancing on the roof. What will the neighbors think? Besides, this time they might make off with the Cow."

"Scare them, you say?" the Old Man asked, shaking violently.

"Yes, scare them."

"But how?"

The Old Woman thought a minute. "Take my biggest pot and a big spoon. Go outside and make a terrible racket. That will do the trick."

"How do you know it will work?"

"It will work. It's an old remedy for witches . . . I think."

So the Old Man got up—even though he really wanted more than anything in the world to stay where he was—because he could not afford to lose a cow as well as a donkey. He got up his courage, took the pot and the spoon, and went out into the yard. There, while the Old Woman watched from the doorway, he began jumping up and down, banging the pot with all his might, and yelling at the top of his lungs.

Alf, when he saw this, was utterly dumbfounded. He had never seen the Old Man act this way before. And for no reason at all that Alf could think of. Had the Old Man suddenly gone mad? Alf stood up in order to see better.

Unfortunately, he forgot all about holding on to the chimney. Just at that moment a great big gust of wind came—and down he went, head over heels, sliding and tumbling from the roof.

The Old Man, seeing something hurtling toward him, rushed inside the house in terror.

Alf landed in the yard in a heap. The Old Folks peered out from a crack in the doorway. All they could see was a shapeless hulk with a pointed top.

"It's a witch!" said the Old Man in a hushed voice.

The shadowy hulk said, "Ee-yonk."

The Old People looked at each other. "A witch with the voice of a donkey?" said the Old Man.

"No, it's Alf," said the Old Woman. "Alf in the shape of a witch."

They looked out in bewilderment, not knowing what to make of this strange state of affairs.

Alf, finding that he was not hurt, stood up and shook himself.

"It's Alf for sure!" cried the Old Man.

"So it is!" cried the Old Woman. "His old self again. You must have frightened the witches so much they decided to give him back to us," said the Old Woman.

"Do you think so?"

"I do. I certainly do," said the Old Woman admiringly.

"Why, so I must have," the Old Man said, pleased. "I must have, indeed. I'll bet they won't be back again. They'll have *me* to deal with if they try anything like that again."

"Ee-*yonk*," said Alf.

Then the Old Folks rushed out and covered his shaggy head with joyful kisses. They brought him inside (for he was shivering with wet and cold) where the Old Man sat him in the rocking chair and covered him with a blanket while the Old Woman made him hot chocolate. And the Dog came and licked his face, the purring Cat came and sat next to him, and the Canary sang with all his heart.

And Alf thought to himself that, although it had been nice being a runaway donkey, it was far nicer to be a come-home-again donkey. He thought that he must love them all very much, because he felt so happy to be with them again. He told them so, too. It came out sounding like this: "Ee-*yonk-yonk*." But they understood perfectly.

He thought also that they must love him very much, the way they were acting. Then suddenly he realized something—if they loved him, that meant he *was* lovable, after all.

From then on, things were much better. It wasn't that anything changed very much. It was true that the Old Woman remembered more often that he liked apples and carrots. It was true that the Old Man remembered more often to rub his rough head gently at the end of a hard day's work. But mainly, Alf was satisfied because he knew now that the other animals worked no less than he, and that he was loved no less than they. And that was just as it should be.

So things went on pretty much as they had before, except that now when the Old Folks went to market, the Old Man was fond of telling everyone the story of how, all by himself, he had scared off two dozen witches who had come to steal all his animals, and how he had stood up to them and forced them to give him back his dear Donkey. And wasn't his Donkey standing right there to prove it?

Whenever Alf heard this, he nearly laughed his head off, because *he* knew there had never been any witches. But since his laugh always came out sounding like "Ee-*yonk*, ee-*yonk*, ee-*yonk*!" no one else was ever the wiser.